THE TRUST WALK

written by Susan Ekberg • illustrated by Michelle Neavill

Father's love is endless...
Always believe –
Susie Ekberg ♡

Spiritseeker Publishing, Inc.
Fargo, ND

Library of Congress catalog card number: 94-92201.

ISBN 0-9630419-6-7

Typeset by Jodee Bock *(thanks, Jode!)*

Printed in Singapore.
First edition.

Spiritseeker Publishing, Inc.
P.O. Box 2441 • Fargo, ND 58108-2441
1-800-538-6415

"Tell us a story, Mommy — of when you were our age, of when you were bad, of when you were scared, of when you were alone . . . ."

"**C**ome, my sweet children, tuck under my arms —
I'll tell of the trust walk that happened long ago . . . ."

The moon was a sliver high up in the sky. Father and I walked to the edge of the forest. I tried hard to see, my eyes scrunched up like this, but there was no moonlight to help with my quest. I shivered a little, half excited, half scared — it now was my turn, and I wanted to be brave.

Father explained it to me one more time. 'Now I'm going to stay right here at the edge, and you will walk down on that path all alone. Just see how far that you can go. And if you get scared, always remember — I'll be right here.'

I took a big breath and started to walk. One step, two steps, I thought I'd be fine, then darkness crept in on me.

I couldn't see in front of me, beside me, behind me. I knew I must still be on the path — that made me feel better. But not much.

'Daddy,' I squeaked in a tiny mouse voice, 'are you still there?'

'Yes, honey, I'm right here.' His words cut through, like a flashlight's beam. I stood up tall, breathed a breath, and walked out further into the unknown.

I sighed a little, shook out my arms,
then listened —
to crunches, twitters and shuffles.

I smiled. I knew the raccoons,

the skunks,

And deer. I saw them in daylight —
I knew they were gentle and not to be feared.

But, oh, in the dark, there could be

WOLVES . . .

Or **BEARS** . . . or who knows what else, in the forest at night? Maybe something that never was seen before . . .

Something huge and black with bright shining eyes?

Or something not seen, but only just heard?

Growling and snarling and showing its teeth . . .

sniffling and snorting and smacking its lips . . .

bigger and **bigger** you *knew* it
was there, but when you turned to find
it . . .

It would just disappear?

Then you'd hear it behind you —

arms reaching out   toward you?

The 'what-ifs' grabbed hold of me, furry and hot, and held me so tight that I just couldn't breathe . . .

'DADDY!'

I screamed in my highest of voices.

'ARE YOU STILL THERE?'

His words boomed out over the tops of the trees,

filtered

through

leaves,

then

settled

on

me.

'Yes, yes, honey — I'm still right here.'

I started to cry — from
relief or from fright . . .

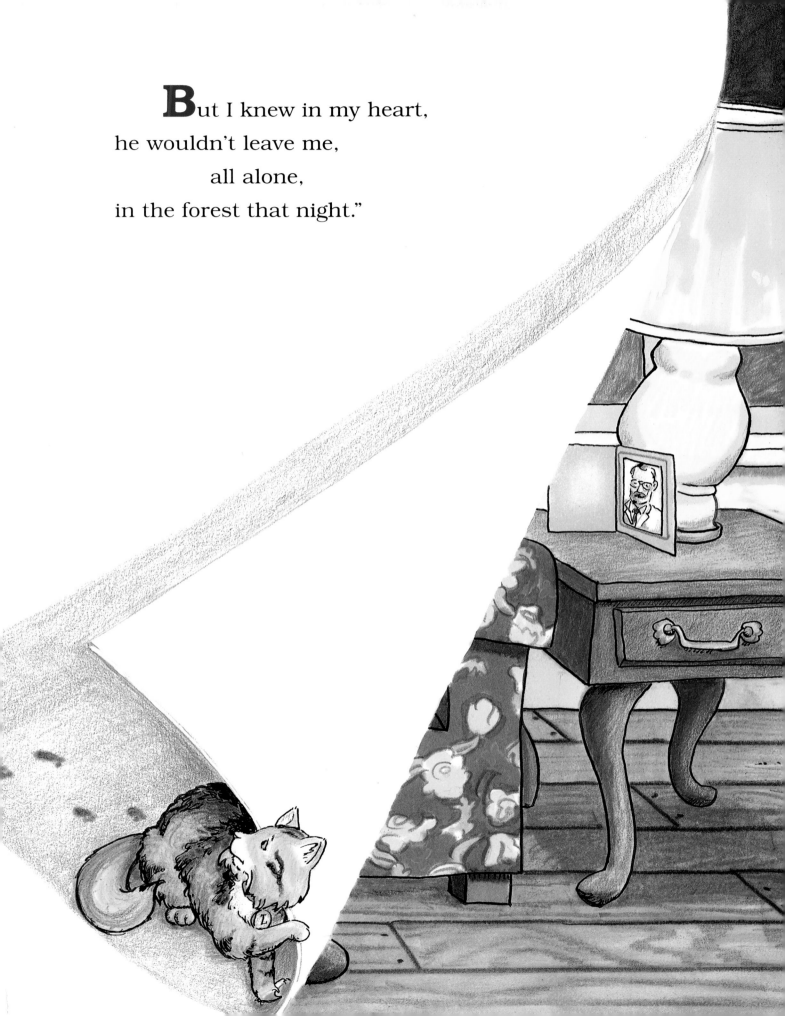

But I knew in my heart,
he wouldn't leave me,
all alone,
in the forest that night."

"**B**ut how far did you go into the forest that night?"

"You sounded so scared, did it turn out all right?"

"Good questions all, my sweet little ones. But my journey didn't end on that dark summer night. I walk in that forest every day of my life. The "what-ifs" still grab me, wolves and bears, they surround me. They haunt me and hunt me 'til I've nowhere to run.

So whenever I'm scared, when it feels funny right here, I stop, and I listen. I think of my father, and his words heard that night . . .

'**D**on't worry, honey, I'm still right here . . .'

then I know it's all right."

This is a true story of an experience with my father in Blackduck, Minnesota, when I was seven years old. Although it was a scary thing, it also was wonderful, and had a great impact on me, teaching me about love and trust. How would I have felt if Dad had left me, all alone, maybe thinking it funny? Would that have affected my view of the Universe? Shaken my trust? But he **did** stay, and I trusted him. He stayed, and I knew he loved me, and loves me still.

William Alan Ekberg

Unconditional love is the common thread that weaves through my writings. If we don't feel it when we're young, we look for it for the rest of our lives, hoping that others can give it to us. But it really is deep down inside us, as the One who will never leave us, who loves us, and stays with us. So though we may look for it everywhere else, it's right there inside of us, where it's always been, and where it will stay — Father calling to us from the edge of the forest —

"Don't worry, honey, I'm still right here . . . "

Thank you for that gift, Dad — given from a father to his daughter on a moonless night — I love you.